The Adventures Of
Annie

Sagarika Priyadarshanee

INDIA • SINGAPORE • MALAYSIA

ISBN
Paperback 9798889596592
Hardcase 9798896326496

Acknowledgement

My writing journey was born from the chaos of unexpected life events that turned my world upside down. I'm grateful for the unwavering support of my loving sister, who stood by me through thick and thin.

I'd also like to thank my dear friend, who introduced me to the captivating world of anthologies. Their presence in my life has been a game-changer, and I'm forever grateful.

My parents have been my pillars of strength, offering guidance, encouragement, and unwavering support throughout this journey. I'm thankful to everyone who believed in me and helped shape me into the person I am today.

This science fantasy book, my third solo project, holds a special place in my heart. It follows the journey of Annie, a brave adventurer who embarks on perilous quests to save the worlds. I've poured my heart and soul into this novelette, allowing my imagination to run wild and free.

1

A thunder-like sound jolted me awake. I checked the clock on the bedside table; it was half past midnight. My room was completely engulfed in darkness. So, I squinted my eyes to see through the dark. Suddenly, I noticed a bright light emanating from beneath my bedroom door. Wrapped in my blankets and holding them closer to me, I walked up to the door and opened it slowly. Blazing white light blinded my eyes, and I found myself being sucked into the void.

I woke up suddenly and found myself in total darkness. There was not a single ray of light to be seen. I was scared to death, my legs were shaking, and my whole body was shivering with fright. Then I saw some light moving towards me. I realized it was a small butterfly-like fairy. Then a swarm of fairies followed. The entire place lit up, and I realized that I was in a dense forest, as I could see huge trees surrounding me.

The fairies started showing me the way, urging me to move forward. I followed them all the way. They went in one direction, spreading their light all over the place. I followed them to an ancient and secluded mansion. After a moment of contemplation, I shuffled towards it and suddenly found myself falling into a dark crevice. I fumbled along the way desperately trying to hold on to something concrete but in vain. After some time, I landed on the wet ground with a loud thump. I groped wildly in the darkness.

But then, I saw the fairies coming to my rescue. They started showing me the path ahead. I looked around and found myself inside a tunnel. There was nothing more I could do but follow the fairies.

I continued walking, completely oblivious to the danger that lay ahead. After a while of walking tirelessly, I came to a halt in front of a staircase. I looked up and saw it spiraling up and up as long as my eyes could see. Then I decided to ascend the steps and began climbing the staircase. It felt like an eternity going up, and I was hopelessly exhausted; my feet were sore and my head was reeling.

After ascending a thousand or so steps, I saw a door in front of me. I turned the knob of the door slowly, and my heart started beating faster with each passing moment. As I opened the door, a loud screeching sound nearly scared me out of my wits. I walked in and found myself standing right in the middle of a gigantic chamber full of antique pieces and several various kinds of artifacts. I could do nothing but gape at the marvelous architecture of the chamber. One could easily tell that it was a centuries-old mansion just by looking at the interior. *Perhaps I should explore some more.* I went about the room but couldn't find a single door.

My eyes landed on a weird statue of a girl holding a teacup. I started walking towards it, but the lights went out, swallowing me in darkness. I guess, I tripped over something, perhaps, the rug and fell onto the statue. The teacup moved and rotated slightly, and then, to my astonishment, a door popped up from nowhere. The door was, however, emanating vibrant light that lit up the chamber. I turned the knob and opened it. Then, I found myself standing in a corridor, and paintings were hanging on the wall that stretched on forever. A gust of wind blew through my hair, and I suddenly started feeling cold. But I noticed there were no windows from which wind could come in. As I was brooding over it, a grinding sound made me look backward. And my jaw dropped to my knees. A skeleton was waddling towards me, its bony hands outstretched as if to strangle me. A quiver shot through me, and the hair on the back of my neck stood on the end. I ran to save my dear life and came across a staircase that would take me downstairs. Glancing back a little, I saw the skeleton still pursuing me. Without a second thought, I hurried down the stairs and reached the bottom of the staircase breathless. I put my right hand on my chest and huffed for more air. Then, I looked up to check on the skeleton, but it disappeared and was nowhere to be seen.

I looked around, gyrating on the same spot, and discovered myself in a huge hall where a magnificent chandelier was dangling from above. Then I noticed a painting hanging on a wall draped in a red linen cloth. I walked up straight to the wall, removed the cloth and threw it aside. There was a beautiful portrait of an elegant-looking woman, who was wearing an ebony-colored velvet, shimmery gown and holding a black cat in both of her hands. A silver crown embellished with precious stones and gems adorned her head, a total contrast to her dark attire and black cat. Nonetheless, she was looking absolutely gorgeous, and I concluded her to be the Queen of this massive mansion. I might just have infiltrated a palace without knowing about it. And I had no idea about the kind of trouble I had gotten myself into. Perhaps, it was just a misapprehension or something, but I saw the eyes of the portrait Queen blink a little and her lips curved into a thin smile which was enough to creep me out.

After pondering the incident for a minute, I decided to explore the mansion a little and embarked on a mission to find some more information about the Queen. She'd already stirred a certain amount of curiosity within me through her stunning yet mysterious appearance. Something was just not right about her, and I couldn't figure out what.

After wandering through the halls and corridors for nearly an hour or so, I reached an enormous library where thousands of books were kept on shelves that almost touched the ceiling. As I watched, an ancient-looking book fell to the ground, emitting a soft glow. I approached it cautiously, but just as I did, someone appeared out of nowhere, blocking my path. I stumbled backward, losing my balance.

That someone, extended his hands to hold mine, but it passed right through my hand, and I hit the floor with a thump and passed out.

When I gained consciousness and opened my eyes, I saw someone crouching right above my head and looking down at me. I sat upright and tried to move away from that person. He was wearing a quaint princely attire with a smile etched on his face. I literally fumbled for words and was speechless.

"Are you okay?" he asked.

"Huh... I... Umm. Who are you?" I asked him finally.

"Hello! Young lady. I am Prince Daniel," he replied courteously.

"I'm Annie."

"This palace belonged to me years ago," he continued. "Well, now that I am dead, I am no longer sure if I can exercise my right to this palace. But the fact is that I still live here as a ghost."

"Wait, did you say you are dead?" I inquired, horrified.

"Yes. I'm extremely sorry for not being able to save you from falling," he apologized. "See, I am trapped in time, and I can't touch a single thing outside my time period. You belong to the present time, so it's impossible for me to touch you."

Saying so, he extended his hands towards me. I flinched and backed up a little.

"You don't have to fear me. I won't hurt you," he pacified. "I have been trapped in this palace for years now, and only you can free me. Therefore, I sent the portal to bring you here."

"Me. I didn't understand a thing you were saying. How can I free you?" I asked him.

"Only you can free me from the curse. Because you are the one the portal chose, and the book never lies," he said with confidence.

"What portal?"

"The portal, do you remember the brightening light that brought you here? That's the portal."

"And what about the book? Wait a second..." I pointed towards the book still lying on the floor. "You're saying about that book which was like glowing a while ago."

"Yes, 'The Book of Eternal Magic', which holds the answers to all the questions existing in this world," he said, picking up the book.

<h1 style="text-align:center">2</h1>

He explained to me that the book said only the one with a pure soul and a kind, courageous heart has the power to defeat the evil queen. When I asked him about the queen, I came to know she was the woman in the portrait I had seen before. Then he told me the whole story. The Queen, however, was a witch, who entered the kingdom and became the guest of the palace after helping the prince's mother using some unusual tactics. She intended to acquire the prosperous kingdom and its wealth, as well as to discover the secret that was kept well hidden for centuries. Therefore, she seduced the King into marrying her after forcing Prince Daniel's mother, to jump off a cliff, which resulted in her death.

So, as a matter of fact, the Queen was the Prince's stepmother. Initially, she was good to all but as time passed, her true colors were revealed. One day, the prince finds out the reason behind his mother's untimely death and decides to avenge her death by punishing the evil Queen. He kept a steady watch on her, gathered every possible evidence against her, and presented it before the king, who immediately condemned her to death. The enraged queen cried her crocodile tears and succeeded in killing the king with her evil magical powers. But before she could murder the prince, he captured her in a portrait using his powers, which he learned from his grandfather. However, the queen was clever enough to cast a spell on the palace, leading to its doom as well as the prince's demise.

"So, you're saying that you know how to perform real magic, aren't you?" I asked him after he finished his story.

"Yes, that's right. I was tutored by my grandfather at a very young age," he replied. "He taught me all sorts of magic."

"Your grandfather taught you magic?"

"Yes. Our ancestors dealt with magic and sorcery. But it was always for the betterment of our kingdom and its people. Once, one of my ancestors was exiled to the depths of the forest, wherein he met a sorcerer from whom he learned sorcery and magic. He acquired a magical ring and a spellbook, which further enhanced his powers. After that, he returned to his kingdom, took back his throne, and punished the one who betrayed him. Thereafter, the teachings and the secret were passed down to the next generation and so forth. Especially to the successors and the to-be emperors until..."

"Okay, that was quite a story," I said, genuinely amazed. "Let me sink all that in."

"I trapped the queen in the portrait, but soon she will be free, ready to create havoc once again," he said and sighed. "And only you can stop her."

"No, I don't think I can. I mean, I'm just a normal college-going girl," I retorted. "How can I stop an evil Queen? It's impossible."

"You are saying this because you don't know your worth yet, Annie," he said.

"My worth? I'm neither a hero nor a warrior," I argued back.

"You are special and that's why the portal chose you and no one else," he asserted, confidently.

"No, I am not."

"Oh, yes. You are. And you proved it already by overcoming all the obstacles that came your way. You passed the test."

"Passed the test? Wait. What test?" I was surprised.

"Your test began as soon as you fell down the hole and landed in the cavern."

"Gosh!"

"Followed by the staircase, then the chamber you found yourself in, ending with the skeleton chaser conjured up by me."

"Why on earth did you do all that? Do you even know how scared I was?"

"I did all this to check out your potential. And I must say you passed with flying colors."

"Oh, my God! I can't believe this."

"Pardon me for that. But I did send the fairies to show you the way."

"And the fairies did a good job. But still, I can't believe you did all this only to check my capabilities."

"You should know what you are fighting against. The evil Queen, who is really cruel and power-hungry. I needed to be certain it's you who can defeat her, which I am now."

"I am not sure if I would be able to do it. I am afraid, I would let you down."

"You have it in you. The courage, endurance, and wit needed to defeat any evil being. You just need to believe in yourself."

"Okay, I'll try with all my heart."

"A little advice from my side- Never underestimate the power of your enemies."

"Oh, I'll definitely take care of that."

"But first, we have to locate the magical ring and the book of spells as well. Also, unearth the secret that lies beneath this huge mansion."

"Let's go then. Why are we still here?"

"But, I guess, you need to change your outfit first."

We strode through the corridors and hallways until we reached the farthest and secluded corner of the mansion. He took out a wand from beneath his robe and continued to draw something on the wall that vaguely resembled a key. Suddenly, the wall transformed into a door, and he pushed it open. Then he walked through the door and gestured for me to follow him inside. It was dark, and I couldn't see anything. He lit up the place with his wand, revealing a well ahead. I walked to the well, peeked down, and saw a staircase leading down and down into more darkness.

"Oh, no. More stairs," I grumbled.

"Don't worry, Annie," he said and chuckled. "Just come around here."

He jumped over and landed on his feet on the first stair. I followed him and did the same as soon as he went down the second stair. A moment later, the stairs began to descend automatically like an escalator.

"Woah. This is spectacular," I exclaimed, completely awestruck.

"This is called magic. I told you there is nothing to worry about," he said.

"Yeah."

"You are going to deal with a hell of a lot more magic from now on," he warned. "So brace yourself for the greatest adventure of your life."

"I really hope this greaaaatest adventure of my life doesn't end with my doom," I murmured.

The staircase swirled down slowly like a snake, taking us down with it. I jumped out of the last stair as soon as the staircase hit the bottom and landed on solid ground. There was an opening up ahead, from which white light was coming in. He moved forward and urged me to follow him closely. I sauntered along with him, passing through the white light into a dense forest. I was shocked to see it was broad daylight, and the sun was shining high in the sky, basking us in its light. I looked back to where we came from, and my eyes popped open. There was a huge tower standing upright, almost touching the sky.

"What in the world is this?" I exclaimed. "I think I'm going to conk out at any moment."

"I informed you earlier that you are going to encounter indefinable magic from now on."

"Yeah, but this is a bit too much to handle, Daniel. Umm, I mean, where exactly are we?"

"This place was built by my ancestors for the safekeeping of the mysterious ring and the spellbook. And this magical place is just underneath the mansion."

"Underneath the mansion? You've got to be kidding me."

"No, of course not. Do I look like I am kidding?"

"Uhh, there is a whole sky above. How can this be under the mansion?"

"I told you this place is magic. Anything can happen. Magic doesn't have any limitations."

"That I can clearly see. But what are we going to do now that we are here?"

"It's simple. Complete the quest without getting yourself killed."

"Wait, what? A quest?"

"Yes. I am here to accompany you on your mission. My magic won't work here, however."

We started striding onward and towards acquiring our target under the vast canopy of trees looming over us. As we walked along, neither of us spoke. After some time, the earth beneath us began shaking and trembling. "What on earth is happening?" I whispered. But then, before my eyes with a massive rumbling, the earth started parting ways, and lo! There was a rift between the two halves almost instantly, like partners separating after a huge brawl. The worst part was, it took me along with it. The ground beneath my feet gave away, and I fell into the cavity created by the rift. *Perhaps, this is the end.*

Immediately, a hand shot down and held my right hand. I looked up and saw Daniel holding my hand. He pulled me up slowly and carefully to save me from getting any bruises.

"Umm, thanks for saving my life," I said with gratitude. "But how? I thought you couldn't touch me," I added, confused.

"I thought so too," he replied. "But after noticing you tumbling down, my hand went ahead involuntarily to help you out. Apparently, things work differently here," he added after pondering a little.

"The real question is, how are we going to cross over this massive rift and reach the other side?" As soon as I asked the question, a loud voice echoed from somewhere. I looked around for the source of the voice, but couldn't find any.

"Where is this voice coming from?" I cried out.

"I am the Guardian Angel," the voice boomed, "here to guide you throughout your journey here. I will ask you a riddle and the right answer will take you one step closer to your destination."

"I don't know if I'm clever enough to solve the riddles," I said to Daniel.

"Have patience, Annie," he whispered. "I know you will figure it out somehow."

"Here is the riddle," the voice said,

"White when dry, black when wet,

It has its home in the sky,

Blown by the winds it cries where it rests,

You can see it dangling above your head,

In the cold hilly terrain."

I tried very hard to decipher the riddle, and at last, the right answer occurred to me.

"Clouds," I shouted out loud and clear as if my whole life depended on it, which was somewhat true, of course.

"Correct answer," the voice declared. "And now a little gift for you."

"I told you. You can do it," Daniel said, smiling from ear to ear.

Soon after, small chunks of clouds lined up one after another, forming a bridge between the rift. I hopped onto the first cloud, and it felt like a soft pillow under my feet. I started jumping from one chunk of cloud to the next, with Daniel following close on my heels. When I reached the middle of the clouds bridge, I lost my footing and balance. As I was about to fall off the cloud chunk, he clutched me from behind and steadied me. I offered my thanks and resumed my hopping.

Finally, we reached the endpoint of the bridge and then jumped to the other side.

I saw a gate emerging from the ground, along with fences on both sides. The gate opened automatically, and we walked through it. All I could see was sand everywhere as far as my eyes could see.

"What is this place?" I asked and answered my own question, "We are in a desert, aren't we?"

"I think so. It definitely looks like a desert. Let's walk."

Having no other option available, we trudged ahead.

3

After walking for a mile or so, I grew weary and all my energy seemed to have drained out of my body. The heat was unbearable, and my throat burned with thirst. I yearned for some water to quench my thirst, but it seemed impossible to find any. Suddenly, I saw a pond. It felt as if I had gotten my life back, and I started running towards it. I think he tried to stop me or something, but I didn't pay heed to what he was saying and continued running in the direction of the pond. Maybe, it was just my imagination, but the pond itself appeared to be running away from me. Confused, I stopped in my tracks. Finally, he caught up with me and started yelling at me.

"What the hell were you doing?" he asked, glaring at me.

"I was thirsty, and I saw a pond over there." I pointed.

"There is no pond. Look."

And to my horror, there was no pond. I was chasing a phantom pond the whole time. A few moments later, I stared at him as his expression turned to one of sheer dread. I turned back and saw a sandstorm approaching us at a tremendous speed. We ran in the opposite direction as fast as our legs could take us.

"I don't reckon you should be terrified of a sandstorm or anything," I shouted while running faster than an athlete in a marathon. "I mean, you're dead already."

"I'm not worried about myself. I'm worried about you."

As we were fleeing the sandstorm, the sun too was setting on the horizon. I stumbled upon some object and fell down. He helped me to stand as fast as he could, and then we continued running. The sandstorm was approaching rapidly, and I was breathing heavily. And I think I saw something that could save us, but I had my doubts.

"Is that a pyramid up ahead, or it's just my imagination like before?" I asked, and he looked in the direction I pointed.

"Oh, my God, it's a Pyramid!" he said happily as if he somehow managed to defeat death.

We scooted towards the Pyramid and found the door bolted shut. "What are we going to do now?" I raised a question. Then, I noticed a carving on the right side of the pyramid wall which looked familiar. I gazed down at the object I was clutching in my hand, and to my utter astonishment, it resembled the carving. As soon as I shoved the object inside the carving, the door glided sideways, revealing an entrance. We rushed through the opening quickly, and the door closed behind us.

"What the hell just happened? How did...?" He broke off.

"You remember I stumbled and fell midway."

"Yeah, and I had to pick you up before the storm could swallow you whole."

"Very funny. It looks like the object I stumbled upon saved our lives, uh, my life. I picked it up while you picked me up."

It was somewhat dark inside, but enough light for us to discern the silhouettes of the surrounding walls. He found a lantern fallen in a corner and tried to make it work. It did work after some idle tinkering with it. The place was filled with dull light, enabling us to see the path ahead. We walked onward, creating shadows on the wall. Soon we found out that we were crossing the same path again and again without actually going anywhere.

"I guess, we have been here before," I said.

"Yeah, I think so."

"We are inside some kind of maze, aren't we?"

We inspected the place for some clues, and I discovered a brick carved in the shape of an arrow. As per my suggestion, we followed the arrow to see where it led us. We reached the corner and searched the walls for more arrows. After following the sculptured arrows for a few minutes, we finally reached the center of the maze. There was a chest kept on the top of a squared stone pillar nearly 3 feet tall. I walked towards it carefully and examined it with my eyes. The maze walls disappeared into the ground with a thundering sound. Something was written on the lid of the chest in a language I couldn't understand.

"Daniel, there's something written over there," I said. "But I can't decipher it."

"I can read it, though," he said. "The text is inscribed in an ancient language. 'The chest can only be opened when moonlight showers itself upon it.' That's it."

"Moonlight! Are you serious? This entire place is sealed. Not a single opening or a window to be seen anywhere. From where do we get the moonlight to fall upon it?"

"There has to be something. We need to find it, together."

A few moments later, I got exhausted and sat on the floor. My eyes fell on the side of the stone pillar where a stone had a moon symbol engraved onto it. I scrambled towards it, and as soon as I touched the symbol softly, it began to glow. A trapdoor opened up somewhere on the top of the pyramid. Soft moonlight entered through the opening, hitting the chest directly. I could see the full moon shining in the sky so far yet so near. The lid moved up, revealing the secret hidden inside. I saw a small box-like thing kept in the center of the chest. Upon Daniel's insistence, I picked up the box.

"We did all this hard work for a stupid ornamental box," I said, disappointed.

"Nothing is stupid here. Each and everything we find is of great significance."

"Okay. Okay," I said and rolled my eyes.

"Whoa," I shouted as the floor under my feet filled with sand. The entire floor filled with sand before my eyes shortly after. Hastily, I put the box inside the pouch and tied it around my waist. He held my hand tightly as we started sinking into the sand slowly.

"What is happening? I'm going to die," I shouted in a panic-stricken tone.

"Absolutely not," he assured.

I was entirely immersed in the sand and then discovered myself in the water. He was still holding my hand. I thrust upwards by pushing my feet downwards and came out of the sea. The waves were crashing on the shore swiftly. I shook my head in awe as we made our way to the beach, where a castle stood up proudly with all its towers and turrets.

"Now what?" I asked.

"We go in," he said.

As I was admiring the huge, elegant castle, we were surrounded by the castle guards. They chained us and took us through the castle gates. We passed through several towers, gardens, and passageways until we reached a massive hall where a king was sitting on a golden throne. I could do nothing but gape in confusion. The whole incident happened so quickly that I couldn't understand what the hell was going on.

The main guard addressed us both as dangerous trespassers and went to the extent of giving us a spy tag. He ordered us to bow before the king. Daniel kneeled, asking me to follow him.

"Who are you? What are you doing on my premises?" the King boomed.

"I...uh...we," I stammered stupidly.

"You are spies from the kingdom of rebels. If only I could find the Red Flames. Well, it's a start."

"The who?" I asked, surprised.

"You're highly mistaken," Daniel said, proceeding with caution. "We are definitely not spies. And we don't even know who or what the Red Flames are."

"Liars! They are lying, Your Majesty," the guard asserted.

I implored desperately to the king that we were not spies. Tried to convince him that we landed up here coincidentally, but all my efforts were in vain.

"Put them in the dungeons. Their fates will be decided tomorrow at dawn," the king ordered the guards to put us in the underground dungeons until the next sunrise. The guards dragged us through the dark underground passageway and locked us up behind iron bars. We were inside a dank cell with a tiny window high up.

"What is all this?" I asked in frustration. "Do you have any idea about this Red Flames thingy?"

"I am afraid not. My guess is, probably they are a rebel group hiding somewhere."

4

There was an old man locked up in the cell in front of us. That old man said that the king was not the rightful heir to the throne. After the death of his elder brother, he was given the responsibility of taking care of the kingdom and his niece, his brother's only daughter, until she came of age. But on the day of his niece's coronation, the king transformed her into a statue and threw her in a river. Then, he took over the throne as there was no one else to claim the throne and ruled viciously.

Upon sunrise, the guards burst in through the iron bars and presented us before the king.

"Take them out and feed them to the dragon in the cave as an offering," the atrocious King commanded.

"What?!" I blurted out.

Daniel glanced at me. I recalled his words: everything here happens for a reason. Thus, I kept my mouth shut. The guards took us through the paths that cut through the mountains and vast grasslands until we reached an enormous cave. We were being literally thrown into a dragon lair, where the dragon could scorch me to death any moment. Of course, I was slightly terrified, but at the same time excited to see a dragon in real.

"Are you afraid?" he asked, slightly worried.

"Yeah, a little bit. Dragons, I've only read about them in books, but now I'll get the chance to see them with my own eyes."

I could hear the flapping wings of the dragon as it circled above us, spitting fire through its mouth occasionally. I was dazed momentarily, witnessing the massive creature. Then, all of a sudden, it decided to attack us; therefore, it swooped down on us gracefully like a predator who hunts its prey. I swerved left and right to save myself from being crushed and burnt alive. At a point, I stumbled and fell. The pouch dropped, and the small box slipped out of it. I picked up the box and saw the latch was slightly open. The dragon was rapidly closing in on me. Thinking of nothing else, I moved the latch upward, opening the box. A sweet, melodious tune emerged out of it and flooded the whole atmosphere with its music. The dragon stopped dead in its tracks and crouched like some pet animal. Daniel helped me get up by extending his hand towards me.

The ground shook, and several branches erupted, turning into a small bush-like structure with a golden crown adorning its top surface. Daniel urged me to pick it up; hence, I picked it up, my eyes fixed on the dragon, afraid it would get ferocious and attack me at any second.

We emerged out of the cave unharmed, unburnt, and alive, which especially applied to me. Daniel took the crown and scrutinized it thoroughly.

"Do you have any idea to whom this crown belonged?" I asked.

"Huh, I don't...," he started but was interrupted by approaching footsteps. We were surrounded by weird-looking people holding bows and arrows. Daniel instinctively stepped in front of me, the crown still in his hands. An arrow came shooting at him, which passed through him swiftly and struck me just below my right shoulder. I touched the wound with my right hand and felt the blood oozing out. Blackness shrouded my eyes, and I most probably fainted after that.

When I partially came to my senses, I saw Daniel carrying me in his arms, and I think we were in a boat. The arrow was absent from my body. Perhaps, Daniel pulled it out. The boat was moving down the river swiftly. A faint sound of water falling down rang in my ears. A waterfall, perhaps. I saw it all with half-opened eyes and wanted to say something, but no words left my mouth. The boat anchored near a rock. Daniel carried me up in his arms and hopped onto the rock. There was a series of rocks leading to the waterfall. We passed through the waterfall, where the cascade drenched me completely. Then we emerged from the cascade absolutely dry. *How is it even possible?* My eyes closed, and I fell unconscious again.

I opened my eyes and looked up at the sky. Then I sat up and let my eyes wander around to find out more about my whereabouts. Possibly, I was inside a garden; I could see a variety of flowers blooming everywhere. A water fountain added to its beauty. Miraculously, the wound below my shoulder had healed and disappeared altogether.

"Are you all right?" I heard Daniel say.

"Yeah, I'm fine. But where on earth are we?" I inquired while trying to explore the place.

"This is the Kingdom of rebels 'The Red Flames' which the king was going on about," he replied. "I walked around and saw trees and huts scattered sporadically here and there. An entire civilization holed up amongst the wilderness."

"How are you feeling now?" a lady draped in a yellow and red outfit asked. She was holding a scepter.

I looked at Daniel for answers.

"This is Lady Sandra, leader of 'The Red Flames' clan. Uh, she healed you."

"Well, I was wounded by one of them."

"I am extremely sorry on behalf of my people," she apologized.

"They thought you were stealing the crown of our beloved Princess, so they attacked you."

"Stealing the crown of your Princess?" I asked, flabbergasted.

"Our Princess," she said, and I turned in the direction she pointed her fingers.

There was a beautiful statue of a Princess standing on a platform surrounded by various rose plants. In fact, she had a crown of roses over her head. Beautifully carved pillars stood elegantly. Colorful birds flew and chirped.

"The Princess!" I exclaimed, "The rightful heir to the throne whom the present king turned into a statue."

"Yes. There was a prophecy that a girl would come, one who would have the power to bring the princess back to life. She would be the girl who could control the dragon and procure the magical crown. My people saw the musical box in your hands after they shot the arrow and realized you were the girl, the savior of the Princess."

A man brought a tray covered in a red cloth and rose petals. The crown was sitting on it.

"Take the crown and put it over the Princess's head," Lady Sandra instructed politely.

I looked at Daniel, and he nodded his head in approval. I picked up the crown, walked to the statue, and then replaced the rose crown with the golden crown. Slowly, the statue melted away, and the Princess came to life before my eyes. Lady Sandra and her people bowed before their Princess in unison. The Princess offered her gratitude to me after I was introduced to her by the Lady.

"I owe you my life. Say, what can I do for you?" the Princess asked me.

"I...uh, we are looking for something, but I have no idea where to find it," I said.

"I know what you're looking for," Lady Sandra said to me.

"Princess, allow me to return your debt," Lady Sandra asked the Princess for her consent. And the Princess agreed to it.

Lady Sandra ordered one of her people to bring some water in a vial from the fountain. Then she ordered another to bring a golden fish from the same fountain in a fishbowl. After all that, she told us that she'd gladly take us to our destination. She asked us to follow her, so we embarked on a path that cut along the vast grasslands, mountain slopes, and valleys until we came across a lake that stretched horizontally from us. I had never seen nature as much as I did in a few hours.

"What now?" I asked.

"You need to dive into the lake," Lady Sandra said.

"What?" I exclaimed. "I don't know how to swim."

"Take this." She handed over the vial to me. "Drink it. This magical liquid from the fountain will help you breathe under the lake water."

As per her instructions, I gulped down the magical water in a jiffy. At first, I slightly hesitated to jump into the lake, but I had to do it anyhow because there was no other option. Hence, I went ahead and plunged myself into the water. When I found myself going down and down, I flapped my arms and legs to and fro. Panic took hold of me as I found myself surrounded by water everywhere. Daniel floated beside me and cupped my face in his hands. Then, he blinked his eyes, asking me to calm down. Shortly after, I could breathe under the water without any difficulty.

A shimmering and shining golden fish swam towards us. Lady Sandra had informed us earlier that the magical fish from the fountain would show us the way. Hence, we followed the fish which was sent to guide us and show us the path leading to our ultimate destination. A few minutes later, the fish came to a sudden halt. I wondered why the fish was not going any further. I extended my arms in a forward motion and felt my hand slip right through the water.

We swam through it and found ourselves in a small cave-like structure that was underwater but completely dry inside. The water is cluttered outside the cave. We walked down the path carefully until we reached a small arena wherein the magical ring and the spellbook were kept on a table. My eyes were fully fixated on the ring as if it was calling me towards it. Everything else disappeared, and I walked towards the magical ring in a rather hypnotized state. As soon as I picked it up along with the spellbook, the whole place disappeared, and I found myself standing in front of the tower, right where I started. Daniel was standing beside me.

"Ready to start the fight against the evil Queen?" Daniel asked.

"I guess so," I replied.

"It's time for you to wear the ring, Annie. Wear it. Let me see how it looks on your finger."

"Oh!" I exclaimed, and slipped the ring onto my right-hand middle finger. It fit perfectly. Nothing magical happened, at least not yet. But I could sense the ring's power somehow. Then it hit me: the real power wasn't in the ring, but inside me. The ring was merely a tool to add to and channel my inner power.

And we were back inside the tower, climbing our way up to the mansion. Fighting the evil Queen was my destiny, I knew that by then. It was a tough task to do, but I had already been through a lot to reach here at this particular stage. As soon as we reached the corridors, a burst of loud laughter bellowed from somewhere in the hall. It was the evil Queen, of course. She was already out of the portrait, waiting for us to come. I had the spellbook and the ring in my hand. A flock of crows came out of the blue and started attacking me. I tried to ward them off with my hands, trying out the power of the ring. But nothing happened.

"These silly crows!" I cursed out loud.

5

The spellbook fell from my hands onto the floor and opened. The pages flapped automatically, as if driven by some strong winds. I bent on my knees and tried hard to pick it up. A spell started writing itself in the book. I read the spell out loud. As I held the open book in my hands, the crows started pouring into it one by one as if sucked in by some unknown force and disappeared. The book ate the crows.

"Whoa! What's just happened?" I asked Daniel. But he was nowhere to be seen. "Oh, my God. Did the book eat Daniel too?" I thought out loud and laughed at my silly joke. But on a serious note, where had Daniel disappeared, I had no idea about that. Next, there came a skull swooshing at me, hovering above my head and making shrill sounds. My ears felt like bursting. The sound made me feel nauseous. I opened the spellbook and captured the skull inside it. I went downstairs and saw the evil Queen standing right in front of me. She was the replica of the portrait. Finally, the time had come to face the evil Queen and defeat her once and for all.

"You have come to face me, little girl. Look at me. You think you can defeat me. What a shame!" she declared and laughed hysterically.

"Don't you think you are kind of underestimating me?" I exerted.

"Underestimating you! Before long, the entire world would be beneath my feet, and I would rule all. You tiny girl can't do anything to stop me."

"As long as good is there, evil cannot win," I proclaimed.

"Let's see," she declared openly.

She shot out a tiny ball of magical light towards me, and I tried to block it with my ring, shouting the spell out loud. A circular magic ball, a sphere-like thing, surrounded my whole body which protected me from the Queen's magical attack. It worked. I felt the power churning inside my entire being. I attacked her with the same force, but she easily deflected it away. She was powerful enough. I would give her that. The thing is that I was missing Daniel. *I mean, how could he disappear in a moment like this?* However, our duel continued. I was full of energy, but the evil Queen was powerful as well as smart and clever. Something happened. She did something different this time. She extracted power from somewhere and said it would freeze me forever. She directly tried to hit me with that powerful force, but at the exact moment, Daniel appeared before me with a large mirror in his hand. The force hit the mirror and reflected at the Queen. She froze. I was horrified and confused.

"Daniel, where the hell have you been?" I asked him, fear etched onto my face.

"If it weren't for this mirror, you would have been frozen by now," Daniel said. "I went to fetch this magical mirror. I knew something of this sort was likely to happen."

"What is this? A magical mirror," I asked with piqued interest.

"A mirror which can reverse the spell for a few minutes. Be ready to banish the Queen to hell. She could revive any moment now," Daniel advised.

I opened the spellbook and asked for the right kind of spell. It appeared right in front of me. The evil Queen came back. But before she could do anything, I brandished the ring out and shouted the spell. A powerful force arose from the ring and hit the evil Queen. She was absorbed into the book and banished to hell for good.

I looked at Daniel with tears in my eyes. I smiled deep from my heart. At long last, the evil Queen was defeated and driven away to the place she belonged to.

"It's time for goodbye, I guess," I said.

"Yeah, you did really well. I am so glad," he said.

"It wouldn't have been possible without your help. You were there with me throughout." I showed my gratitude. "Umm... What about the ring and the spellbook?"

"They're yours. Keep them with you," he said.

He conjured up a portal directly into my room, and I went through it. I felt something for him. It was really hard saying goodbye to him. Nevertheless, he was dead, and it was just his spirit I interacted with the whole time. I hid the spellbook inside my closet and kept wearing the ring on my finger.

6

A few days later, I went to the supermarket to run some errands. I had to buy some groceries out there. After I finished buying, I bumped into someone and some items fell from my bag. That person helped me pick up those things. He was wearing a cap, so at first, I was unable to recognize him. But then, when I saw him clearly, I was dumbstruck. That boy exactly looked like Daniel. I couldn't understand what was happening. Perhaps I was hallucinating or something.

Somehow, I tore my eyes away from him, went outside, and started walking down the pavement. A car pulled along beside me. The same boy offered me a lift. I was utterly confused, but I took the risk. I got myself inside the car.

"If you don't mind, can I ask you something?" I said after hesitating for a moment.

"Yeah, go on," he said expressionlessly.

"You look like somebody I know. But it's somewhat impossible. How? I don't know what I'm asking. I'm sorry. I am a bit confused," I said finally.

"Don't be. Because you are right. I am that somebody. I am Daniel. Although, now I prefer to be called Danny," he said.

"What?! How?...," I stammered.

"I will explain it to you, but before that, I want to confess something. I love you," he said confidently. I only stared at him speechless.

He explained to me that when we went to find the ring and the spellbook, Lady Sandra had given him an elixir that could bring a spirit back to life. He drank it later that day when I left after defeating the evil Queen. Now, he had regained his life and was very much alive. That elixir was also hidden there by his ancestors. He confessed that he had feelings for me and wanted to spend the rest of his life with me. He came back for me. I revealed my own feelings, telling him I loved him deeply. We were overjoyed. He also mentioned that after coming back to life, he retained his powers. He still had his wand with him.

We went through the forest, and he stopped the car in front of the mansion. The mansion was kind of invisible to the eyes of others. We went inside and had the day of our lives. We were together. He used a magical powder, and sprinkled it all over us, which made us fly. We flew around and had lots of fun.

This was just the beginning of our adventure together. I had the magical ring and the spellbook, and it was time to test some spells. We imbued a globe with magic and created an anywhere globe. It could take us anywhere in the world. We just had to think about the place and put a finger on the exact place, and lo! We stood in front of our destination. We traveled to new places like Paris, France, Florida, Switzerland, New York etc. using that globe. Explored parts of the world.

We could visit each other's minds by using spells from the book. Danny's mind was jumbled. He had countless memories stacked away in various things. We explored some of them. I literally went inside his memory and saw as the things happened. It was exciting. Then we visited my mind. My memories were in the form of books. I opened a book and both of us entered my memory lane.

7

The days passed by and we did the unthinkable. We accidentally opened a portal to a new world while trying out some spells. Danny and I were magically transported to the new world. There were black rocks and mountains dangling in the sky here and there, but very far away. "Floating mountains," I thought out loud. No houses were seen anywhere on the ground. Trees were there, but sporadically. This did not look like our world. It was definitely some other world.

"Danny, did we do something wrong?" I asked, horrified. "Where are we? This place is different."

"This does not look like Earth," he said. "Maybe we are on a different planet."

"A different planet? How are we supposed to go back?"

"Let's try a spell from your spellbook. Hopefully, it will send us back."

I asked the spellbook, and a spell appeared, but when I said it, nothing happened. We didn't move an inch.

"This is not working," I groaned. "What do we do?"

"We'll definitely find a way out, but first let us explore this place until we find our way back."

We walked for miles but found nothing. Just more mountains and trees. Suddenly, there were sounds above our heads. We looked up and saw small flying machines like fighter jets and flying cars hovering below the dangling mountains.

There was a large flying saucer, too. It confirmed our suspicion. "Alien aircraft," I shouted. "So people are living here."

"Definitely," he agreed.

"Do you have your wand with you?"

"Yes, I've it inside my jacket."

"I also have my ring and the spellbook. What if the people here attack us thinking we are outsiders? We should be ready for their attack."

"I don't know if my magic will work here, and I am not sure if the spellbook and the ring will work either."

"But we have to try in case..."

At that time, some of the flying machines left their troop and came swooping at us. They all landed around us. Some men, who were wearing armors on their bodies and helmets on their heads came out of the flying machines and strode towards us. I was shivering head to toe due to fear by then. They had blue skin, yet they looked like us. There wasn't much difference between them and humans, except their skin was blue. One of them said something in a language I couldn't understand. I asked Danny about that, and he too couldn't understand. We were in desperate need of a translation.

Danny took out his wand, and they all backed up a little, conferring among themselves. He raised his hand to assure them. He did a spell by waving his wand, and suddenly I could understand them. They were threatened by our presence. They knew we didn't belong here.

"Who are you?" one of the men asked again.

"We...uh...," I stammered, unable to think anymore.

"We are from Earth," Danny answered. "We came here accidentally through a spell, and now we are unable to go back."

"Come with us," that man said. "You need to see our king."

We didn't have a choice but to go with them. We were stuck here, and we had to do what they said. I accompanied a man and Danny accompanied another. They took us to their flying cars. They had advanced technology by the looks of it. Not only that, but they had a device attached to their hands that probably threw laser beams. I hopped onto one of the flying cars, and it ascended slowly. I was seated in the seat next to the pilot's seat.

A few minutes later, we reached our destination. I could see houses, skyscrapers, and people going about their daily lives from above. More flying cars could be seen everywhere. Some forests stretched over the vast lands. There was a big palace in the middle of the huge kingdom. The entire area around the palace was surrounded by fences on all sides and a huge entrance gate to go with it. The flying car landed on a big tower that was situated inside the palace. I came out of it and saw Danny coming out, too.

He came and stood in front of me. "Are you afraid?" he asked with a note of concern in his voice.

"A little," I replied. "Do you remember when the king in our quest ordered his guards to throw us into the dungeons and then sent us to the dragon lair?"

"Yeah, I remember." He smiled. "This feels different. I can sense it. We're on a different planet, I think. And the king definitely won't throw us into a dungeon. Stop worrying so much. Whatever it is, we'll face it together."

"Okay, let's go."

We followed the men who took us down in an elevator instead of a staircase. The guards outside the throne room, took all of us inside, where the king was seated on a big golden throne. His expression gave him away. He was a bit surprised to see us.

"Who are they?" the King asked calmly.

It was my time to be surprised. The king was oddly calm, unlike the king I met before, who shouted angrily after seeing me and Danny.

"They are saying they are from Earth, Your Majesty," one of the men who brought us said. "They came here by mistake through a spell and are unable to go back."

A person wearing a black cape who was standing beside the king said something in his ear. The king looked pleased.

"I welcome you to our planet," the King said and looked at me and Danny in turn. "This is Planet Yuka. We are not so different from you. I assure you of that. But it is situated in a different galaxy than yours. Here, magic, and advanced technology go hand in hand."

"Thank you, Your Majesty," I said. "By the way, I'm Annie and this is Daniel, who goes by Danny."

"I have to confess," he said. "You did not come here mistakenly. We summoned you. This here, my warlock friend, summoned you. He hijacked your spell that brought you here. At first, I was a little surprised to see you because I didn't think it would work."

"What!" Danny and I exclaimed in unison.

"Why would you do that?" I asked.

"We had our reasons for bringing you here," he replied. "You see, there is a huge war going on here. A warlord from another planet came here to start a colony. He wants to capture all of our kingdoms and rule. There are several kingdoms located throughout the planet, and he has captured some of them on the other side of the planet. Those who try to oppose him and his army, he wipes them out from the face of the Yuka. We are one of the kingdoms he hasn't reached yet. But he can attack our kingdom anytime, so we are ready for him. He has indefinable power. He knows mind control and has many powers up his sleeves."

"I understand what you're saying," I said after hearing his story. "But what can we do? Why have you brought us here?"

"We need your help in defeating the warlord. We know you defeated the evil Queen by using your ring and your spellbook. These are the things needed to kill the warlord, among a few other things."

"How do you know that?"

"My friend here knows a spell or two. He was searching for a way to defeat the warlord and came across you two. He learned about a certain ring and a spellbook situated on Earth. And when he came to know about these two things being in the possession of you, he brought both of you here."

"My ring can defeat the warlord?" I asked, dumbfounded.

"Yes, but we need a few other things," the warlock said. "Six ingredients are needed to be mixed and the ring has to be doused in the mixture which will then give it the power to kill the warlord."

"Do you have these ingredients?"

"I am sorry to say, but no," the warlock said, disappointed. "We don't have it. You two have to find it."

"Another quest," I grumbled.

"Something like that," the warlock said, satisfied. "I have a map that will guide you throughout. We also have a compass installed inside the kriptor. That will help you immensely in finding the other kingdoms. I will say the name of the ingredients and show you their pictures, so it will be easy for you to find them."

"Kriptor?" I asked, puzzled.

"The flying machine in which you came here," he replied. "It's called a kriptor."

"So, we'll be traveling in your kriptors?" I asked, fascinated.

"Yes," the King answered. "These cars run on solar energy. So, there is no possibility of fuel running out."

"And the name of the ingredients?" I asked, intrigued.

"Hell flower, the roots of the Caryptus, the tears of the Tamelon, the hair of an old witch, the blood of the Kralope, and the feather of the Sinyx," the warlock answered.

"What are these things?" I asked. "I have never heard of them."

"Wait, let me explain," the warlock said softly. "Hell flower is a red color flower that grows in the enchanted forest due west. Generally, it grows in hell, but it also grows in the enchanted forest near the river of death. As I have heard, it also grows on Earth."

He showed us a picture of a Hell flower.

"What are the roots of Caryptus?" Danny asked.

"Caryptus is a plant that grows in the Kingdom of Dale due north-west," the warlock said and showed its picture. "It is used for medicinal purposes, but the root of the plant has magical properties. It's impossible to find. You have to know what you are looking for. Its leaves are pointed. See."

"What is a Tamelon?" I inquired.

"It is a magical animal that is found in the enchanted sea due north," he answered and showed its picture. "It is like a seahorse that is found on Earth. But it emanates electricity like a jellyfish and is huge. Its tears are precious and have magical properties."

"Where do we find the old witch?" Danny asked.

"She lives in the forests of the Kingdom of Hardle due east," he replied. "She is the oldest witch over 400 years old. She has three strands of golden hair that are magical. You have to bring one strand. She only appears in front of those who need her help. Otherwise, she is very difficult to find."

"What is the blood of Kralope?" I asked. "Do we actually have to bring its blood?"

"Oh, no." He looked amused, chuckled a little, and showed its picture. "It is a magical fruit which is juicy. Its juice is called blood here. You will find it in the kingdom of Sar in the garden of a special person named Lhaas. He will not give you the fruit that easily. You have to be careful around him. And yes, the kingdom of Sar is due south-east from here."

"What is a Sinyx?" Danny asked finally. "It sounds like a bird."

"Yes, it's a magical bird found in the Malci desert due south," he said and showed its picture. "It shows itself rarely. One will come across it if one is lucky. And it's very difficult to bring its feather. They are very protective of themselves. It changes its color periodically. So, it's impossible to say which color it will be when you come across it. A magical map will show you its live location."

"Oh, my God!" I exclaimed and sucked in a deep breath. "My head is reeling. Are you sure we will be able to bring all these ingredients?"

"If anyone can do this, it's you both," the King pacified. "I have full faith in you. You have shown your courage and capacity by defeating the evil Queen of your world. She was cunning and powerful but both of you defeated her. And I have full faith that you can defeat the warlord, too."

"The King is correct," the warlock added. "If I had any doubt that you would not be able to do this, I would not have brought you here."

"You don't have to go on the quest right away," the King said. "Both of you will rest today and tomorrow you can explore our kingdom. The day after tomorrow, you can start your journey. Our men here will teach both of you how to fly the kriptor. Until then, go to your rooms, freshen up, and rest."

8

We went to our rooms and ate some food given to us by a handmaid. The food was delicious. It was different from the food we eat on Earth, but it tasted good. At first, I hesitated a little, but then I ate it after she reassured me. The handmaid's skin was green. They also gave us new clothes to wear. I got an orange maxi/gown dress. Danny got a pair of pants and a shirt. The attire was not so different from the clothes we wore on Earth. We rested that day, and the next day, we went outside the palace.

We walked on foot and explored various places. There was a museum that held various historical artifacts. I noticed one thing; the men's skin was blue, while the women's skin was green. There was a café where they offered us their special drink made of their famous fruit. It was tasty.

"Wow, this is delicious," Danny said and sighed happily. "I have never tasted anything like it."

"You're right," I chirped. "It's like a soothing drink. It calmed me a lot."

"Are you having second thoughts about the quest?"

"No, not at all. In fact, I'm excited."

"It will be different from our previous quest. I don't know what challenges we have to face. I hope my magic wand works this time."

"Together, we'll face all the challenges and win. We'll bring all the ingredients, no matter how difficult it will be."

"I hope so."

After a little exploring, they taught us how to fly their kriptors. It was easy once you got the hang of it. I understood all the mechanisms and practiced a little. I flew it well. At one point, I thought I'd drop it, but then I steadied it efficiently. Danny also learned to fly it in one go. He was more efficient than me. I would give him that. I was tired by the time we went back to the palace, so I went to bed straight away.

The next morning, Danny and I went to the throne room to meet the king.

"I hope you had a great time yesterday," the King said. "Today you are going on your next quest. Best of luck to both of you."

"Thank you, Your Majesty," Danny and I said in unison. "We will not let you down."

"You have to park your kriptor outside the other kingdoms and walk on foot to acquire the ingredients," he said. "It is the only rule because our kriptors are not allowed to enter other kingdoms. However, they can fly above them while passing by. Each kingdom has its own kriptors."

"And one other thing, you have to walk to find the Sinyx after reaching the Malci desert," the warlock said. "It is the only way. Because the bird fears our aircraft and prefers to stay away from them."

The warlock gave us a magical map and some items like a magical pouch that could give us what we wanted and two magical swords for each of us among other things for our journey. The magical map was designed in a specific way. It first will show the directions to the place we were to be headed i.e. the flying route, and after that, the location of the ingredient i.e. the walking route. As soon as we find the ingredient, the map updates to show us the next place and subsequently, the location of the other ingredient.

Danny and I went to the tower where the kriptor was sitting idle.

"I'll drive first," he said.

"Okay," I agreed.

We both went inside the kriptor. Danny took the pilot's seat, and I took the seat next to it. We opened the magical map and traveled west towards the enchanted forest to bring the Hell flower. Danny pressed a button and the kriptor sped up.

"I don't know what we're going to face in the enchanted forest," I grumbled. "I'm sure magic will be on the play. The name 'enchanted' suggests it. We have to be careful and use our minds to separate the truth from the illusions we might face."

"Yeah, you're right," Danny agreed. "The warlock had said we have to face our darkest fears and desires in this quest."

"We cannot fail. If we fail, it will bring about the destruction of this planet as we know it."

"Have you noticed one thing?"

"What?"

"Night and day are different here. When the day comes and the night falls, I cannot understand. I'm losing track of time here."

"Me, too."

We reached the outskirts of the enchanted forest after some time. Danny parked it, and we hopped out. I was bursting with both, fear of the unknown and excitement. After some speculation, we entered the forest finally. Tall trees stretched out to infinity. We strode for several hours following the map but found nothing suspicious.

"Help, help me!" I heard a voice drifting towards me. I somehow recognized it. It was my mother's. But how was it possible? My mom couldn't be here. I was on a different planet, for God's sake. The voice was filled with pain, and I couldn't stop myself from following it. I followed it to the depths of the forest. There was my mom howling in pain. Her hair was dishevelled, and her clothes were torn.

I started running towards her when a group of men holding spears surrounded me. I had my sword with me, but my legs froze. I couldn't move. Danny appeared out of nowhere and fought those men, but they outnumbered him ten to one. He fought valiantly, but a man stabbed him with a spear, and he fell to the ground. I rushed to him, crouched beside him, and held him in my arms. I checked his heartbeat and pulse and found none, which scared me to hell.

Horrified, I shouted his name and told him to wake up, but he didn't move. I started sobbing pretty hard. Someone put a hand on my shoulder, and I looked up. Danny stood towering over me. I looked down and found the corpse of Danny gone.

"What happened?" Danny asked, concerned. "Why are you crying and shouting my name? And where did you disappear? Do you know how difficult it was to find you?"

"You're alive!" I cried and threw myself at him. I hugged him tightly, relieved that nothing happened to him.

"Yes, I'm alive. What happened?"

"I thought you were dead. I thought I heard my mom's voice, and I started running towards it. I saw her in a really bad state. And then, some men came and killed you."

"Well, I'm alive and standing right in front of you. It was just an illusion. Let's go."

We started walking, and a few minutes later, I stumbled on a small rock. When I looked up, Danny was gone. Was it another illusion? I could not tell. I searched for him and found him crouching and sobbing. So I went to him and shook him. He came to his senses and looked at me as though he'd seen a ghost.

"What happened?" I asked.

"You're here," he said. "Then, who was she?"

"Who was who?"

"That girl who jumped into the river. She looked like you."

"Oh, my God. I didn't jump into a river. I'm right here. That was an illusion, I guess. This forest is making us see things that don't exist."

"You're right. Let's continue walking. I think we're near."

After some time, we saw a river. And the Hell flower was blooming right beside it. We walked ahead, but we were caught inside a net that took us up.

"Who would put a net here?" I asked.

"Beats me," Danny replied. "Give me the pouch. Maybe it can give us a knife to cut the net."

I gave him the magical pouch, and he took out a knife. He cut the net, and both of us fell with a loud thump. All of a sudden, demon-like creatures surrounded us. They started attacking us. We fought them with our magical swords and killed each of them. After killing them all, we started towards the Hell flower, but it multiplied quickly. Now, there were thousands of Hell flowers, and we couldn't identify the original one.

A fairy appeared in front of us.

"Thank you, for getting rid of the demons," the fairy said. "They were creating havoc here for years. They had driven us away into hiding. Now we are free."

"It was our pleasure," I said, grinning.

"What can I do for you?" she asked.

"We came here for the Hell flower," Danny answered. "But now we're unable to find the original one."

"I will tell you how to find the right one, but first you have to answer a riddle," she said.

Danny gave me a knowing smile.

"We're ready," I said. "Ask away."

"The thing that flows, but changes its direction. When it ends, it becomes bigger." She gave us the riddle.

I thought about it for some time and the right answer occurred to me.

"A river," Danny and I said in unison.

"Correct answer," the fairy said. "Now sprinkle the water from the river on these flowers. The right one will glow."

"Thank you," I said.

Danny waved his wand and the water from the river started drizzling on the flowers. A flower glowed. That was the flower we needed. I went ahead and plucked the Hell flower. Then, I kept it inside the bag given by the warlock to keep all the ingredients.

We followed the map and came out of the enchanted forest in one piece. There were no illusions on our way back. Soon, the map showed us the location of our next place. We went inside the kriptor and continued our journey to the

Kingdom of Dale for the roots of the Caryptus. The map and the compass, both helped us. On the way, we made a quick stop, took out some food from the magic pouch and ate.

9

After reaching our destination, we parked the kriptor outside the kingdom of Dale and walked. There was a check post at the entrance where they asked about our identities as we looked different.

"Who are you?" a man asked. "Where are you from?"

"We are not from here," I said. "Here, take it."

I showed him the letter given by the king that stated our purpose and our identities.

"A letter," he said. "So, you are from the kingdom of Yres, which is also called the kingdom of magic. Only the king of that kingdom can send a letter." At first, he wasn't convinced, but later on, he agreed to let us in after some thoughtful conversations.

Danny opened the map, which showed us the location of the Caryptus. After walking a mile or so, we finally reached our destination. We stopped outside a store.

"I think, the Caryptus is inside this store," Danny whispered. "Let's go in."

We went inside the store and found no one.

"Hello, somebody in here," I shouted.

"Yes," a lady spoke and came out. "I am the owner of the store. Say, what do you want?"

"Uh...we," I stammered.

She looked surprised when she saw us clearly and eyed us suspiciously.

"You do not look like you belong here," she said. "What brought you here?"

"We want the roots of Caryptus," Danny said.

"Ah! I see," she said. "I have it, but you've got to pay the price. It's not free, and I am not talking about any money."

"What do you want?" Danny asked.

"I am a witch doctor," she said. "People don't come here often. They've lost faith in my methods and medicines, as they now believe in modern science. A long time ago, I had captured a demon who tricked me into freeing him. He's like a Genie of your world. Without him, the faith has gone completely. He is the one who can bring back people's faith. You've got to capture him again and bring him back to me."

"What?" I exclaimed.

"Do it and I'll give you the roots of Caryptus," she declared.

"Where can we find him?" I asked her. "We don't know where he is."

"You'll find him in the Kuzuku forest," she replied. "He is a trellox demon. He has horns; he is grey in color, and he doesn't have any legs. One more thing, he'll try to trick you as he had tricked me. So, be careful."

"You've captured him once. Can't you capture him again?" Danny asked.

"No, he has forbidden me to capture him again," she replied. "I can't do it, but you can do it on my behalf."

She gave us a map that showed us the location of the Kuzuku forest that was situated inside the kingdom of Dale. She also gave us a jar to capture the demon. We agreed to capture the demon for her because we didn't have any choice. We wanted the roots of the Caryptus badly, so there wasn't an option to disagree.

We followed the map and reached the forest. Once we were inside the forest, we took out the fruit given by the witch doctor. She'd said that the fruit was the demon's weakness. He'll come for it, no matter where he is. After some time, the demon appeared before us.

"May I ask where you two are going?" the demon asked.

"We're explorers," Danny said. "We were just passing by, and we were hungry, so we took out this fruit to eat. Doesn't it look delicious?"

"So it is," the demon said and grinned. He looked at the fruit greedily and said, "I want it."

"If you want it, you'll have to come with us," I said.

"What is this?" the demon bellowed. "Is this a trick?"

"No, no, no," Danny said. "We just want you to come with us."

"Not so easily," the demon declared and scowled. "First, you have to play a little game with me. If you want me to come with you, then you have to play hide and seek with me. I'll hide and you have to find me. If you find me, I'll come with you."

"You have to make a blood pact," Danny said. "A promise that can't be broken."

"Okay," the demon agreed.

He cut his palm. So did Danny. Then they shook their bloodied palms. The deal was sealed.

"Before you go off and hide, you have to fight me," Danny declared.

"Okay," the demon said, smiling. "Let's see who wins. The winner gets the apple."

"Agreed," Danny said.

Danny took out his sword. The demon conjured up a sword. They started fighting. At long last, Danny lost.

"I saw," I whispered in Danny's ear. "You lost willingly."

"It was the plan all along," he said.

After the fight, the demon went to hide. Danny took out the map and his wand. He held a piece of cloth. It had belonged to the demon. He used the cloth to track the demon.

"He must be around here somewhere," Danny said confidently.

I could see stone pillars at some distance. Danny looked around thoroughly and went towards the stone pillars. He touched one of them and shouted, "I found you."

The pillar immediately turned into the demon. I was shocked.

"How did you find me?" the demon asked, surprised.

"All the stone pillars had shadows except one," Danny replied casually. "I know a Genie doesn't have a shadow."

"Very clever," the demon said.

Danny took out the jar and the demon went inside it. We returned to the store and gave the jar to the witch doctor. She thanked us and handed over the second ingredient, 'the roots of the Caryptus.' I kept it inside the bag and bid her farewell. She seemed thoroughly pleased with us.

We went back to where we'd parked our kriptor. This time it was my turn to fly it. We continued our journey to the enchanted sea. The magical map showed us the way. We stopped after some time to rest. The next day, I drove again, and we reached our destination. I flew the kriptor above the sea, following the direction of the map. It was the only place that couldn't have a walking route.

I stopped it when we were near. After that, I parked the flying car, and it hung mid-air. We threw ropes down towards the surface of the sea and rappeled out. When we reached the bottom of the ropes, we plunged into the sea. Once we were in the water, we ate the weeds given by the warlock, enabling us to breathe underwater. Holding the map, Danny and I swam towards the location until we saw some people who were half-men and half-fish. Instead of legs, they had the tail of a fish. Merpeople. How was this possible? I thought they were only found on Earth.

"Danny, see, Merfolks," I exclaimed.

"Yeah, let's approach them," he said.

They saw us coming and approached us.

"Who are you?" one of them asked. "What are you doing here?"

"We're looking for something, and I think it's here somewhere," I said cautiously.

"Where are you from?" that merman asked.

"We're from Earth, but we came here on behalf of the king of Yres," Danny replied.

"Then you should see our king," he said. "Come with us."

We followed the merpeople who took us to an underwater castle. They presented us before the king, who was sitting on a throne made of stone. He was holding a trident. A mermaid who looked like his queen was sitting beside him.

"Your Majesty," one of the mermen said. "They come from the kingdom of magic, and they are looking for something. So I brought them to you. They say they are from Earth."

"So you are from Earth," the King said.

"Yes," Danny said.

"Our ancestors are from Earth," he said.

"Your ancestors? Your Majesty," Danny asked.

"Yes, eons ago, at the beginning of mankind, there was a fissure created by an all-powerful warlock that connected this sea to the sea on Earth. Many merpeople and sea animals were sucked into the hole, and they appeared here. The fissure was closed, so they were unable to go back to Earth. So for generations, we have been staying here."

"That's what I was wondering," I said.

"What are you looking for?" the King asked politely.

"Tears of the Tamelon," I replied.

"Tamelon, I see," he said. "For years, that magical animal had terrorized our people. Merman warriors fought him, but they couldn't kill him despite trying for many years. They died fighting. Our numbers started to dwindle, but we still tried hard to defeat it. But it was filled with electricity, and our men couldn't fight it.

"Then, one day, we invited a warlock from the kingdom of magic who put it to sleep. It had been sleeping since then. But it's almost time for it to wake up, and we are scared. We don't have enough men, and we can't afford to fight. If you can help us, we will be highly indebted to you. We will repay you by giving the tears of the Tamelon which our men procured."

"How did you procure it?" I asked curiously.

"I created a bubble around it to keep the water at bay. Then, my men sprinkled some magical water into its eyes, which made it cry. Thereafter, they kept a vial under its eyes, and the tears flowed right into it. We had heard its tears were magical, so we decided to obtain it before the warlock sent it to sleep."

"Okay, we'll try to defeat it," I reassured.

At that moment, a merman came running ---or in his case, swimming---rapidly. Utter terror was etched on his face.

"Your Majesty, the Tamelon woke up and is coming," he said and huffed. "As usual, it is creating havoc and destroying everything in its way."

"Don't worry," Danny said. "We'll do something."

We swam towards the Tamelon. When we reached it, Danny and I took out our magical swords. Then we started attacking it, and it fought back. Electricity couldn't hurt us because Danny had put a protective sheath on us. The king had said it couldn't be killed, so we thought about capturing and trapping it. Danny conjured up a chain and tied one end around its neck and the other end around his own waist. He swam to the farthest part of the sea, and I followed him. There I took out my spellbook and chanted a spell. White light burst from the ring and hit the animal. The magic traveled for miles and trapped the Tamelon within it, creating an invisible boundary. It could never go out of the boundary.

We returned to the castle and told the king that the Tamelon would not terrorize them again. It had been trapped. The king was happy to hear the news. Then he gave us the vial containing the tears of the Tamelon, and I carefully placed it inside the bag. We thanked the king and returned to the place where we'd parked the kriptor. We climbed the ropes and got inside the flying car. Danny drove it to the kingdom of Hardle.

After some time, we reached our destination. We parked our flying car outside the kingdom and went ahead. Danny showed the letter given by the king at the checkpoint, and they let us in. We followed the map, which led us to a forest. The witch must be living inside the forest. The map only showed the location of the forest and not the witch. The warlock had said she lived off the radar. No map can show her. She'd hidden her exact location quite well.

"How do we find the witch?" I asked. "We don't know where she lives."

"I think, I have an idea," Danny whispered. "Do you remember the warlock said the witch only comes out when someone needs her help. We're just going to give her that."

"How?"

"Watch me." Danny took out his wand and conjured up an animal that looked like a wolf but had spots like a tiger and was yellow.

"What animal is this?" I inquired.

"I don't know, but this is a ferocious animal that will attack us anytime now. I'll try to fight it."

As soon as the words left his mouth, the animal attacked. Danny fought it bravely, but got bruises and wounds all over his body. I thought the animal would kill him when an old lady appeared and threw some powder at the animal. It backed off and calmed down, leaving Danny heavily injured. It did not take much time to guess that the lady was hundreds of years old witch.

"Come with me," she said quietly. "I can heal your wounds."

She took us to her cottage and tended to Danny's wounds. She applied some magical paste to his injuries, and they completely healed after mere moments.

"Who are you?" she asked after Danny was healed. "What brought you here?"

"We come from the kingdom of Yres, but we are the inhabitants of Earth," I replied.

"So the king of Yres sent you," she said softly. "What is your purpose, if I may know?"

"We need a strand of your golden hair," I replied. "It's one of the ingredients the warlock sent us to fetch."

"A strand of my golden hair, you say, but it will come with a price," she said.

"We'll pay whatever price you ask," Danny said.

"Listen, a sleep demon has tormented me for years," she let out. "Night after night, he's tortured me with never-ending nightmares. I haven't had a peaceful night's sleep. You have to capture him. He's targeted my cottage. Whoever sleeps in it is afflicted by nightmares. Help me capture him. Then I'll give you my hair."

"Okay, don't you worry," I reassured her. "We'll capture him."

She humbly gave us food to eat. As soon as it was time to go to bed, we went to sleep. Then, the nightmares started. First, I was locked inside a coffin. No matter how hard I tried to get out, I couldn't. I shouted, "Let me out." But nobody listened. I pushed at the cover of the coffin, but it didn't open. I didn't know that it was all a dream. Everything seemed pretty real, so I was afraid I would die. After some time, I couldn't breathe. My eyelids were starting to close when the coffin flew open.

I scrambled outside the coffin and huffed for more air. I found myself inside a house and went to the door so that I could get out of the house. As soon as I was out, I fell down. The house was hanging in the sky. I screamed as I went down. After what seemed like hours, I crashed into the water. It looked like a sea. I swam in a random direction when I saw a large shark swimming towards me. Within seconds, I was in the shark's stomach.

I died and was resurrected on a street. I started walking, but I was run over by a speeding car. Then, I searched for my house, but couldn't find it. At long last, I found it and went inside and heard the ticking of a clock. It was coming from under the table. When I went to look, a bomb exploded and turned me into ashes. After that, I saw Danny. A hooded man had put a knife to his throat. If I didn't do anything, the man would kill him. I walked ahead and stumbled. A box came out of my bag. I remembered everything. The box had been given to me by the witch to capture the demon. It could travel during sleep.

"Go ahead, kill him," I shouted. "I do not fear you."

The hooded man sliced Danny's throat, and I stood there motionless. I didn't utter a single word. The demon appeared before me.

"Why are you not screaming?" he asked. "Are you not afraid?"

"No, I am not afraid," I replied. "Now it's time for you to go inside the box."

I opened the box, and the sleep demon was pulled inside it. I had captured the demon. Then I opened my eyes and saw Danny crouching beside me.

"What happened?" he asked expectantly. "Did you catch the demon?"

"Sure did," I replied. "The demon is inside the box."

The witch thanked us and gave us a strand of her golden hair. I kept it inside my bag. We took our leave and went towards the place where we'd parked our kriptor. We hopped inside, and I drove towards the kingdom of Sar. Once we reached our destination, we followed the map, which took us to the home of Lhaas. It was a huge mansion. The gate was open so we went inside.

Near the door, there was a door phone. A man answered when we called. As soon as we introduced ourselves, the door opened. A servant welcomed us in and took us to a huge chamber. Someone was sitting on the sofa near a fireplace. When we went in, he stood up and turned towards us.

"Hello there, dwellers of Earth," he said. "I am Lhaas. It's my pleasure to meet you."

"You look different from the people who stay here," I said slowly. "Your skin color is somewhat purple, and as far as I've seen, the men's color is blue and the women's color is green here."

"A thousand years ago, some of my ancestors came here," he started. "My ancestors were space explorers. Due to some technical failure, their spaceship caught fire. Some took pods and fled to the nearest planet, which turned out to be planet Yuka. They couldn't contact anyone because they had left their planet to look for other habitable planets. They had nowhere to go, so they stayed here."

"That's quite a story," I said. "So you are from a different planet?"

"Yes," he answered. "Now, what can I do for you?"

"We came here in search of a fruit called Kralope," Danny replied. "We heard that it is in your garden."

"Yes, you're right," he said. "It grows only in my garden because the sapling was brought here by my ancestors from my planet. When they fled, they were able to gather some things. Kralope tree is magical. Wherever it grows, it fills the area with magic. The nearby trees come to life. I will give you the Kralope, but first you have to pass a test."

"We're ready," Danny and I said in unison.

He ordered his servant to bring two chalices.

"These are two chalices filled with magical water," he said. "You have to drink from one chalice and the other has to drink from the other. There is poison in one, and the other can fulfil your greatest desire. Choose the chalice you want."

I thought about my greatest desire. I always wanted to be the student of the year at my college. But now I had Danny. My priorities had changed. If I have to die to let Danny live, so be it.

"I choose the one with poison," I said hastily.

"No way, I'll choose the one with poison," Danny interrupted. "You give the other chalice to Annie."

As soon as these words left his mouth, he took the chalice from Lhaas's hands and gulped down the contents. Shock rippled through me. I waited for Danny to clutch his throat and fall any moment. But nothing happened.

"Both of you passed the test," Lhaas said. "It was a test to see who is willing to die for the other person. Now, I permit you to go into my garden. The fruit Kralope is waiting for you."

"Thank you," Danny and I both said.

We went inside the garden, which was situated in the backyard of the mansion. After some walking, we found the tree. Before we could pluck it, branches from other trees came at us and started to bind us.

"Before you take my fruit, you have to agree to a condition," the Kralope tree said.

"A talking tree?" I wondered out loud.

"What condition?" Danny asked.

"Only one of you can touch the fruit and pluck it," it said. "The person who plucks the fruit is free to go, but the other one stays back."

I thought for some time and whispered something in Danny's ear.

"But first, free us from these binds," Danny said.

"Okay," it agreed.

All of a sudden, the branches freed us. Danny sat on his haunches, and I climbed on his shoulders. Then he stood up. I extended my hands towards the fruit and plucked it.

"Now you have to let both of us go," I said confidently. "I plucked the fruit with Danny's help. Your condition was fulfilled. Danny didn't touch the fruit, but he still helped me in plucking it. So, in a way, both of us plucked the fruit without Danny touching it."

"Very good," it said. "Both of you can go now."

I tucked the fruit inside the bag. We got the fifth ingredient. We followed the map to where we'd parked our kriptor. Then we continued our journey and sped towards the Malci desert. We parked our kriptor on the outskirts of the desert and walked. Walking on the sand was a difficult task, but we had a little experience because of our previous quest.

We walked for hours following the directions on the map. I held the map. The spot that showed the bird glowed. There was a sound of flapping wings. When I looked up, I saw the Sinyx. It was different as it was green this time. The warlock had said it changed colors. It had to be the Sinyx because the map couldn't be wrong.

"Danny, look up," I exclaimed. "It's the Sinyx."

"What?" He looked up. "Show me the map." He took the map from me and agreed.

"We have to follow it," Danny said. "Let's see where it is headed."

We followed the bird until it flew above a huge rock mountain.

"Do we have to climb the mountain?" I groaned.

"No, that's not necessary," he whispered.

He waved his wand and wings sprang out of my back. He grew wings, as well.

"Now, this is cool," I said excitedly.

We flew up and landed on the surface. I was dumbfounded, witnessing the scene before me. The Sinyx had a nest perched on the mountain. A man with a head of a snake was in a close battle with the Sinyx. As much as I could tell, he was trying to steal the bird's egg. There was a portal just a few feet away. He might have fled with the egg if not for Danny. He grabbed the snake-man from behind and spun him around. The snake-man hissed.

Danny managed to snatch the egg from him and threw it towards me. I jumped and caught it. It was a nice catch, I must say. Danny started fighting him, but the snake-man caught Danny by the throat and lifted him up. Danny shoved at his face and hand, but couldn't free himself of his hold. I thought he'd die.

"Danny, the knife," I shouted.

Hearing that, he took out his knife and drove it right through the snake-man's heart. His grip loosened and he crumpled to the ground. Danny threw the corpse inside the portal and the portal closed. Heaving a sigh of relief, I put the egg in the nest where it belonged.

"Thank you," the Sinyx said gratefully.

"You can talk?" I asked, only slightly surprised.

"Yes," it replied. "What can I do to return your favor?"

"Can you give us your feather?"

"Yes, take it."

It shredded one feather. Suddenly, it turned orange. It had to be the original color of the bird. I kept the feather in the bag, mumbled a thank you and flew down, with Danny following me closely. Once we reached the ground, the wings disappeared. We walked back to the kriptor, hopped into it, and drove back to the Kingdom of Yres, following the magical map and the compass.

10

Upon reaching our destination, I gave the bag containing all the ingredients to the warlock. He prepared for a ritual. In a dark room, he drew circles with candles around it. In the middle, a large bowl was kept. There was water in it. Danny, the king and I stood at some distance. The warlock chanted spells for some time and then took the bowl out. Thereafter, he added the ingredients inside the bowl. As for the Kralope, he ripped out its cover and squeezed it. The juice was red. Hence, the name 'blood of the Kralope'.

He kept the bowl in the middle and chanted another set of spells.

"Give me the ring," he said to me.

I did as he said and waited. He put the ring inside the bowl and chanted another spell. The air filled with an electric charge. All of a sudden, a tremendous force of magic burst out and pushed us a few feet backwards. It lasted like that for a few minutes. The bowl glowed, emitting golden light. Then he took out the ring from the bowl and handed it to me.

"Now, the ring has the power to defeat the warlord once and for all," he said.

The time for the battle arrived sooner than we thought. The warlord came to visit the king.

"Will you consider surrendering before me or do you want to fight against my large troops?" the warlord threatened.

"We are not going down without a fight," the King replied with confidence.

"You want war, so I will give you a war," the warlord declared. "Let's fight. Prepare to lose like those other kingdoms."

We prepared for the ultimate battle. The king had sent secret letters to other kingdoms, requesting that they send their troops, as this was to be the final war between the warlord and us. They were aware that we possessed a weapon capable of defeating him.

The war began on the battleground outside the kingdom and in the air above it. The warlord was, perhaps, inside his spacecraft, monitoring their attacks. Warriors with laser beams and laser weapons fought the enemies. Danny and I were inside the fighter jets shooting laser beams at our enemies. We were connected through comms. Warriors from other kingdoms increased our numbers. Every warrior was fighting valiantly.

We came to know that an evil warlock, who had been banished, had joined hands with the warlord. He was the same warlock who had sent the snake-man to fetch the egg of the Sinyx. Without the egg, his ritual failed, but he was trying hard to defeat us. Our warlock was engaged in a magical battle with him. He might be strong, but our warlock was the strongest.

The warlord was hiding inside his spacecraft, so Danny and I decided to sneak into it somehow. After some careful planning, we managed to sneak into it. Some of their troops were on the spacecraft. We fought them while searching for the warlord. While fighting, my spellbook fell and Danny picked it up. Finally, we found him in the main control room. He snarled at us.

"How did you come in here?" he growled.

He ordered his men to kill us. But we defeated all of them.

"Argh," he shouted. "Have you come to kill me?"

"Yes," I replied with certainty.

"You can't kill me," he cackled.

He turned Danny against me. I knew that he could control minds. Maybe that's what he did to Danny. Under his influence, Danny started attacking me, so I had to fight him. While fighting Danny, I urged him that his mind was stronger than the warlord's influence. If he fought hard enough, his mind would be free. My tactics worked. Danny threw the spellbook at me and took out his wand.

I was wearing my magical ring. He engaged in a magic battle with the warlord to distract him from our original plan. I opened the spellbook and a spell started writing itself. While the warlord was busy fighting Danny, I chanted the spell out loud and brandished my ring towards the warlord. White light shot from the ring and hit him squarely in the chest. He started burning and turned into ashes in no time. Then the ashes were sucked into the spellbook. We managed to defeat the warlord finally.

Once the warlord was defeated, his men started to leave the battleground and flee. Hundreds of warriors had died, but their deaths did not go in vain. We had won. Our warlock had also managed to defeat the evil warlock and trapped him inside a magical well. After the battle was over, Danny and I met the king in the throne room.

"Thank you, Danny and Annie," he said gratefully.

"You are welcome," Danny and I said in unison. "It was our duty to help you."

"This would not have been possible without you," he continued. "The kings of the other kingdoms have sent you their regards. I have decided to throw a ball. All the Kings and Queens, Princes and Princesses want to meet you personally."

On the day of the ball, we met everyone. They thanked us for our valor. Danny and I danced to the music. And like that, it was time for us to leave planet Yuka. I opened my spellbook, which showed us a spell to go back. The warlock also recited a spell. The magic of both the spells mixed and opened a portal to Earth. Earlier, he'd locked us with a spell, and therefore, we couldn't go back to Earth. We said our goodbyes and went inside the portal.

On the other end of the portal was the mansion of Danny. We realized we had arrived at the exact time we'd left. He hugged me tightly and kissed my forehead.

"How did you manage to free me from the influence of the warlord?" he asked, his eyes gleaming.

"I didn't do anything," I replied. "Our love did that. Have you not heard that love can break all the curses?"

About the Author

This is Sagarika Priyadarshanee, from Rourkela. She is the author of 'Swirling Water and Lavender' and 'Sapphire - A collection of love chronicles.' She has embarked on a journey to find peace by writing her heart out. She doesn't think a great degree is needed to become a writer. Just being passionate about her work is the key and learning the art of writing as life goes on. She loves to explore different genres of the writing universe. Writing became her ultimate savior and helped her survive the darkest of days. And she can't ignore the fact that she never wanted to be a writer. She believes in destiny; today, she is here because her destiny steered her here. She loves reading novels based on horror, fantasy and the supernatural.

A little naïve, she lacks a little confidence but once she puts her head into something, she tries her level best to achieve it. Hard work pays off and it's the truth. An introvert who found a best friend in her diary. Initially, she wrote when she was upset but slowly it turned into a hobby. And now writing had become her passion and love. And she would say it took a toll on her but made her who she is today.

Instagram id - @estranged_waves

Instagram id - @sagarika_priya